A Michael Neugebauer Book
Copyright © 1987, Neugebauer Press, Salzburg, Austria.
Published and distributed in USA by PICTURE BOOK STUDIO Ltd, Saxonville, MA
Distributed in Canada by Vanwell Publishing, St. Catharines, Ont.
Published in UK by PICTURE BOOK STUDIO, Neugebauer Press Publishing Ltd. London.
Distributed in UK by Ragged Bears, Andover.
Distributed in Australia by Era Publications, Adelaide.
All rights reserved.
Printed in Belgium by Proost.

LIBRARY OF CONGRESS CATALOGING IN PUBLICATION DATA

Hoffmann, E.T.A. (Ernst Theodor Amadeus), 1776-1822
The nutcracker
Translation of: Nussknacker und Mausekönig
Summary: After hearing how her toy nutcracker got his ugly face,
a little girl helps break the spell and changes him into a handsome prince.
[1. Fairy tales] I. Zwerger, Lisbeth, ill.
II. Bell, Anthea. III. Title.
PZ8.H675Nt   1987   [E]   87-15249
ISBN 0-88708-015-0

Ask your bookseller for these other PICTURE BOOK STUDIO books
illustrated by Lisbeth Zwerger:

THE GIFT OF THE MAGI by O. Henry
THE NUTCRACKER by E.T.A. Hoffmann
THE NIGHTINGALE by Hans Christian Andersen
LITTLE RED CAP by The Brothers Grimm
THE STRANGE CHILD by E.T.A. Hoffmann
HANSEL AND GRETEL by The Brothers Grimm
THE SEVEN RAVENS by The Brothers Grimm
THE SWINEHERD by Hans Christian Andersen
THUMBELINE by Hans Christian Andersen
THE LEGEND OF ROSEPETAL by Clemens Brentano
THE DELIVERERS OF THEIR COUNTRY by Edith Nesbit
THE SELFISH GIANT by Oscar Wilde
THE CANTERVILLE GHOST by Oscar Wilde
A CHRISTMAS CAROL by Charles Dickens

E.T.A. Hoffmann

THE NUTCRACKER

retold by Anthea Bell
illustrated by Lisbeth Zwerger

PICTURE BOOK STUDIO

It was after dark on Christmas Eve when little Marie and her brother Fritz had their Christmas presents – for presents are given on Christmas Eve in Germany, where Marie and Fritz lived in the last century. They had some wonderful presents, too: dolls, toy soldiers, picture books, and a beautiful toy castle their godfather, old Mr Drosselmeier, had made them. However, the present Marie liked best of all was a nutcracker in the shape of a dear little man with a funny, kindly face, and dressed in fine clothes. She was very sad when her brother Fritz, playing roughly with Nutcracker, broke his jaw. Marie tied poor Nutcracker's head up in her handkerchief, and nursed him for the rest of the evening, sitting on in the living room with all the toys after the rest of the family had gone to bed.

Just as Marie put Nutcracker away in the toy cupboard, the clock struck twelve. And on the stroke of midnight, some very strange things began to happen. Mice came out from behind the skirting and up through the cracks in the floorboards: a whole army of mice led by the terrible great Mouse King, who had seven heads. Then all the dolls and soldiers and the other toys came to life. Nutcracker himself drew his little sword, waved it in the air, and shouted, "My loyal subjects, will you stand by me in battle?" "Yes, sir, we'll follow you to death or glory!" replied the toys. Under Nutcracker's command, the toys fought a great battle with the mice. At last, however, Nutcracker was driven right back to the glass-fronted toy cupboard, with only a few of his soldiers. The Mouse King himself scurried up, all seven throats squealing triumphantly. Nutcracker was in great danger, and Marie, watching, couldn't bear it any lon ger. "Oh, poor Nutcracker!" she sobbed. Hardly knowing what she was doing, she took off her left shoe and threw it into the middle of the mice, aiming at their king. Then everything swam in front of her eyes, she felt a pain in her left arm, and she fell to the floor in a faint.

When Marie woke she was lying in her bed, with the doctor and her mother beside her. "Oh, Mother, have the nasty mice gone away? Is Nutcracker all right?" she whispered.

"Now, Marie, you mustn't talk nonsense!" said Mother. "What a fright you gave us! You must have stayed up so late playing that you felt sleepy, and when something startled you, you put your arm through the glass in the toy cupboard door and cut yourself quite badly. I found you on the floor there, with all the toys lying around you. Nutcracker was beside you, and your left shoe was on the floor a little way off." And when Marie tried to tell her mother and the doctor about the great battle they wouldn't believe her, but said she had a temperature and must stay in bed for a few days.

Poor Marie was very bored, but one evening Godfather Drosselmeier came to see her and Fritz. To her delight, he brought her Nutcracker back, with his jaw mended. "But he's not the most handsome of fellows, you must admit," said Godfather Drosselmeier. "If you like, I'll tell you how the Nutcracker family came to be so ugly! Have you ever heard the story of Princess Pirlipat, Mistress Mousie the witch, and the Watchmaker? It's called the Tale of the Hard Nut."

Some months before the birth of Princess Pirlipat (Godfather Drosselmeier told the children) her father the King invited some other kings and princes to a great banquet of sausages. The Queen herself made the sausages in a big golden pot, and the moment came when fat bacon for the mixture was to be cut up and fried in silver pans. As the bacon began to sizzle, the Queen heard a tiny voice whispering, "Give me some of that bacon, sister! I'm a queen too, and I'd like to join the feast!"

The speaker was Mistress Mousie, who claimed to be Queen of Mousolia, and held court under the kitchen stove. "Come along, Mistress Mousie," said the kind Queen, "and you may have some of my bacon." But Mistress Mousie's seven great, rough sons came out too, fell upon the bacon, and ate nearly all of it. When the sausages were served, the King was in dismay. "Not enough bacon!" he gasped, vowing to be revenged on Mistress Mousie for stealing it. And he called in his Court Watchmaker, whose name (said Godfather Drosselmeier) happened to be Drosselmeier just like mine, and who made some clever little mousetraps to catch Mistress Mousie's seven sons. One day, while the Queen was cooking her husband's supper, Mistress Mousie reappeared. "My sons are dead!" said she. "So take care the Mouse Queen doesn't bite your own little princess in two!"

When Princess Pirlipat was born, there had never been a prettier baby. Her little face was soft and pink and white, her eyes were bright blue, and she had shining, curly golden hair. Everyone was delighted except for the Queen, who worried over Mistress Mousie's threat. She had Pirlipat's cradle very closely guarded. Two nurses had to sit beside the cradle, and by night there were six more nurses in the room, each holding a cat on her lap, stroking it all the time to keep it awake and purring, for the Court Astronomer had said this was the only way to keep Mistress Mousie away.

One night, however, one of the nurses woke from a deep sleep. All the other nurses and the cats were asleep too - and a huge, ugly mouse was standing on its hind legs with its dreadful head on the Princess's face. The nurse leaped up, with a cry of horror, the others woke too, and Mistress Mousie scuttled away. Little Pirlipat began wailing miserably. When the nurses looked at her, they were horrified. Her angelic, pink and white face had changed to a fat, shapeless head on a tiny shrivelled body.

The King and Queen were dreadfully upset. The King blamed it all on the Court Watchmaker for catching Mistress Mousie's sons in his mousetraps, and decreed that he must find out how to restore the Princess to her old shape, or he would be beheaded.

With the help of the Court Astronomer, the Court Watchmaker discovered that the spell on the Princess would be broken if she ate the sweet kernel of the Crackatuck nut. It must be bitten open by a man who had never shaved, and never worn boots, and he must give her the nut with his eyes shut and take seven steps backward without stumbling before he opened them again. So the Watchmaker set out in search of the Crackatuck nut. He had been on his travels for fifteen years when he went to see his cousin, a dollmaker, and told him his story. To his surprise and delight, the dollmaker had the Cracka-tuck nut itself in his possession, and the dollmaker's son, young Drosselmeier, who had never shaved or worn a pair of boots, was just the man to open it. But there were other young men too who wanted to try cracking the nut, since the King had promised his daughter's hand in marriage to anyone who could do it. Nobody could crack its shell, however, until young Drosselmeier tried - and then the Princess ate the kernel, and became beautiful again. But Mistress Mousie appeared once more, tripped young Drosselmeier up as he took the last of his seven steps backwards with his eyes shut, and turned him as ugly and wooden-looking as the Princess had been before. He was just like a nutcracker! "Oh, take that ugly Nutcracker away!" cried Princess Pirlipat. And he was thrown out, but the Court Astronomer consulted the stars and saw that young Drosselmeier could still break the spell if he defeated the seven-headed Mouse King – Mistress Mousie's son born after the other seven were dead - and found a lady to love him in spite of his ugliness.
So that is the Tale of the Hard Nut (said Godfather Drosselmeier).

When Marie could play in the living room again, and saw Nutcracker in the toy cupboard, it suddenly struck her that the tale her godfather had told must be Nutcracker's own story. Of course! He was really her godfather's nephew, who had been bewitched by Mistress Mousie - for she felt quite sure that the Court Watchmaker was Godfather Drosselmeier himself. And she told herself that Princess Pirlipat was a nasty, ungrateful girl.

Not long after this, one moonlit night, Marie was awakened by a strange sound in her bedroom: a pattering and a squeaking and a whistling. Then she saw the Mouse King coming through a hole in the wall. He scurried around the room, his eyes and his crowns all sparkling, and then he jumped up on Marie's bedside table, squealing, "Teehee! You must give me your sugar plums and marzipan, little girl, or I'll eat your Nutcracker up!"

Next evening, Marie put her sugar plums and marzipan down at the foot of the toy cupboard – and they were gone in the morning! But soon the Mouse King was back, demanding Marie's collection of little sugar dolls, and another night he said he must have her books and her nice new dress. Marie was in despair. "Oh, Nutcracker, how can I help you now?" she said, picking her Nutcracker up. "Even if I do give the Mouse King my books and my dress, he'll still want more!" But to her amazement, Nutcracker grew warm in her hand. "If only you can get me a sword, I'll do the rest!" he told her, before he turned to stiff, cold wood again.

"I can give Nutcracker a sword!" said Fritz, when Marie had told him the whole story. And they took a silver sword off one of his toy soldiers, and buckled it on Nutcracker.

Marie could not sleep that night for terror, and about midnight she thought she heard a great many strange noises in the living room, and a loud squeak. Then there came a soft knocking at her door, and a little voice saying, "Don't worry, dear Marie! Good news!" Putting on her shawl, Marie opened the door, and there stood Nutcracker, with his bloodstained sword in one hand. "Dear lady," he told her, "you alone gave me strength and courage to kill the wicked Mouse King!" And he gave Marie all the Mouse King's seven crowns, as tokens of his victory. "Now," he went on, "there are many wonderful things I can show you if you'll just come with me!"

Nutcracker led Marie to the big old wardrobe, where she saw a pretty little cedarwood staircase coming down through the sleeve of Father's travelling coat. They climbed the stairs, and when they reached the top, dazzling light and delicious fragrance met them. They were in Prince Nutcracker's own country, and Marie admired all the beautiful sights as they went over Sugar-candy Meadow, into a wonderful little wood called Christmas Wood where gold and silver fruit hung from the branches, and then on beside Orange Brook, Lemonade River, and past Almond Milk Lake. Next they came to Gingerbread Village on the Honey River, and Barleysugar Town, but still they went on to the Prince's capital city, in a boat shaped like a shell that carried them down a rose-red river.

They landed in a pretty thicket called Sugarplum Grove. "And there ahead of us is the capital, Candy City!" Nutcracker told Marie. In the middle of the city stood Marzipan Castle, a fine sight with its hundred towers shining with lights. Four beautiful ladies, who must surely be princesses, came out and embraced Nutcracker, who introduced them to Marie as his sisters, telling them how she had saved his life. "If she hadn't thrown her shoe at just the right moment, or got me that soldier's sword, I'd be dead now!" he said.

The ladies flung their arms around Marie, and they all went into a hall with walls made of sparkling crystal. The princesses set to work to prepare a delicious meal, using plates and dishes of delicate china, and silver and gold pots and pans. Watching them pressing fruit, pounding spices and grating sugar, Marie wished she could help. The prettiest of Nutcracker's sisters seemed to guess her thoughts, for she handed her a little golden pestle and mortar, saying, "My dear, would you crush a little candy for me?"

So Marie happily pounded away, while Nutcracker told his sisters about the battle… but somehow, veils of silvery mist were rising, there was a singing and a whirring and a humming in the air, and Marie herself rose on swelling waves, higher and higher, up and up…

Bump! Marie fell from a great height. When she opened her eyes, she was in her own little bed, and there stood Mother. "Oh, Mother!" cried Marie. "Where do you think Nutcracker, who is really Godfather Drosselmeier's nephew, took me last night?" And she told her mother all about her adventures, insisting that they had not been just a dream… for after all, she had the Mouse King's seven crowns to show.

When no one would believe her, however, Marie stopped talking about that wonderful fairy kingdom. But she couldn't forget it, and one day, when God-father Drosselmeier was repairing a clock in the house, she sat by the toy cupboard looking at Nutcracker. "Oh, if you were really alive," she burst out, "I know I wouldn't act like Princess Pirlipat and despise you after you gave up your handsome face and figure for me!"

Then there was such a bang, and a jolt, that she fell off her chair in a faint. When she woke up, Mother was bending over her, saying, "Look, here's your godfather's nephew come to visit us!" And there stood a young man, rather small but very handsome and finely dressed. When he was alone with Marie, he thanked her for all she had done in breaking the spell that had turned him into a Nutcracker.

So soon Marie was engaged to be married to Godfather Drosselmeier's nephew, and after a year and a day he sent a golden carriage drawn by silver horses for her. And so far as I know, Marie and her Nutcracker Prince rule the Kingdom of Sweets to this day.

E.T.A. Hoffmann was born in 1776. His Christian names were originally Ernst Theodor Wilhelm, but he changed the third name to Amadeus as a tribute to the composer Wolfgang Amadeus Mozart. As a young man, he studied law, but he preferred the arts as a way of life. He could paint and draw; he became a professional musician as composer, conductor and music teacher; then he took to writing, first music criticism and then fiction. Most of his stories have an element of fantasy in them, sometimes fantasy of a frightening nature. However, THE NUTCRACKER & THE MOUSEKING, first published in 1819, is one of Hoffmann's happiest tales – although even here there is something mysterious and slightly sinister about the character of Godfather Drosselmeier, who seems to move easily from the real to the imaginary world.

Hoffmann died in 1822 at the age of forty-six. Not only was he a musician himself, but other musicians used his stories in their work. The ballet COPPELIA, with music by Delibes, is based on one of Hoffmann's tales; the same story, along with two others and the figure of Hoffmann himself, appears in Offenbach's opera THE TALES OF HOFFMANN; and then there is Tchaikovsky's well-known ballet THE NUTCRACKER, for which the composer used a version of Hoffmann's story that had been adapted into French by the novelist Alexandre Dumas.

Hoffmann's original text is much longer than the English version in this book, but the translation aims to preserve the details of the plot (which are not always quite the same as those familiar to balletgoers from Tchaikovsky), and above all the spirit of Hoffmann the storyteller.

ANTHEA BELL